Changes

Taylor Sapp

Alphabet Publishing

Copyright © 2023 by Taylor Sapp

ISBN: 978-1-956159-31-8 (paperback) 978-1-956159-18-9 (ebook)

All rights reserved.

Our authors, editors, and designers work hard to develop original, high-quality content. They deserve compensation. Please respect their efforts and their rights under copyright law. Do not copy, photocopy, or reproduce this book or any part of this book for use inside or outside the classroom, in commercial or non-commercial settings, except for the use of brief quotations used in reviews. Do not duplicate the file or store the file or a copy of the file in any public electronic storage device for common use. It is also forbidden to copy, adapt, or reuse this book or any part of this book for use on websites, blogs, or third-party lesson-sharing websites.

For permission requests, write to the publisher at "ATTN: Permissions" at info@alphabetpublishingbooks.com

Discounts on class sets and bulk orders available upon inquiry.

Cover Image: Sofia Zhuravets, Deposit Photos

Adapted by Walton Burns

Contents

Before You Read	IV
Changes	1
Glossary	14
After You Read	15
Writing	17

Before You Read

1. What's the most important thing to you in a romantic relationship?

a. physical appearance

b. intelligence

c. humor

d. good personality

e. other: _____

2. Would you rather the person you are in a romantic relationship with is...

a. more attractive than you?

b. less attractive that you?

c. the same?

Changes

"Sorry I was gone so long. It's not like me, is it?" said the beautiful stranger.

John was waiting for his girlfriend Vanessa at a coffee shop. They had a reservation to meet their friends, Jim and Pam, for lunch at a restaurant nearby. John's mind was on something else. Like how to break up with Vanessa. Should he start by saying, "Let's be friends"?

He certainly liked Vanessa (or Vee which she went by). She was kind, smart, and funny. He really liked her personality. But she was also a short and a little pudgy and her nose was a little big. Worst of all, her small, dull, hazel eyes made him think of a rat. He wasn't proud of these thoughts.

He knew he shouldn't care about looks but it still bothered him. Another thing that bugged him was that he never heard any of his friends say anything nice about her looks. Never. The lack of approval from his friends made him feel uncertain, like he could do better. He was no Brad Pitt, but he felt he had settled. "I could do better." It kept popping into his mind from time to time, like an itch that wouldn't go away.

For example, this stranger who was talking to him. She was the most beautiful woman he'd ever seen, without a doubt. If only there was some reality where he was dating a girl like *that!*

"JJ?" The beautiful stranger called him by his nickname, something only his girlfriend said. That was very odd. She was looking at him and smiling as if she knew him quite well.

However, John didn't recognize her at all. She was of medium height with beautiful dark hair, full lips and most amazingly, large, deep and kind green eyes. Her figure looked that of a model's. She was wearing an elegant black dress that showed it off. On one finger of her beautiful hands was a green jade ring that matched her eyes perfectly.

John didn't know what to say. She was so beautiful that he found it hard to speak. All he could get out was a weak, "Oh hello." He glanced around the room nervously, wondering if he might be the victim of some hidden camera tv show.

"Are you ready to go?" she asked.

The woman was so stunning that John felt his senses slowed. It was difficult to think. And the way the girl seemed to know him confused him even more.

"Go?" he asked, struggling to understand what was going on.

She looked at him a bit suspiciously. "You feel okay, JJ? Don't we have a reservation to meet Jim and Pam?"

"What?"

How did she know about the dinner with their happily married friends? This woman must be a friend of Jim or Pam's. He didn't remember her, but they must have met somewhere. Hopefully, he could figure out who she was before she realized he forgot her.

"Sorry, I didn't know you were coming." John said. He was surprised to see her look grow even more suspicious.

"Ha ha. We're already late, so can we joke later? Let's go."

"I'm sorry but I have to wait for my girlfriend. Why don't you go on ahead to the restaurant?"

Where was Vee? She was 15 minutes late. When she did come, it would be very awkward if he were talking to this beautiful woman. Vee was not the jealous type, but it would only be natural for her to be upset if he was talking to this kind of girl. Especially with the obvious interest she seemed to be showing him.

"JJ!" the woman yelled in a familiar way that sounded a bit irritated but also strangely amused, "Stop goofing with me."

That caused John to freeze for a moment. He was always playing jokes on her, playing with her gullibility, the way she believed everything people say. He loved confusing her and spreading misinformation. "Stop goofing with me" was something Vee always said at those moments.

"You're the one goofing with me! Who are you? Where's Vanessa?" He yelled, but his sudden anger surprised her. The look on the woman's face was hurt and shocked. The look was so genuine, it made John doubt himself.

There was only one way to prove it. He couldn't believe he had to do this.

"Let me show you what Vee really looks like."

John pulled out his phone and opened his photo app. As soon as he showed this woman a photo of Vanessa, this strange joke would end quickly. Ah, here was a photo of them from last week!

The phone fell out of his hand and into his cup of green tea.

On the screen was a picture of the two of them at a Red Lobster restaurant on her birthday a week ago. He remembered this photo. But it wasn't the Vee he remembered in the photos: it was the beautiful stranger, holding up a lobster tail and smiling at the camera.

It didn't seem possible! How could the photo have changed?

"What is wrong with you? Stop messing around. We're late to meet our friends!"

This perfect version of Vee wanted him to leave with her. How could he refuse?

Besides he was curious to find out what Jim and Pam would say. Which Vee would they see?

Lunch with Jim and Pam was completely normal. Not once did they make any comment about the unusual change in Vee's appearance.

As they sat at the café drinking lattes, John couldn't help staring at this stunning woman. He was trying to figure out just what was going on. When the girls excused themselves for the restroom, John seized the moment to speak up.

"Vee's a beautiful woman, isn't she?" John said.

"Definitely." Jim nodded.

"Ok, Jim, enough is enough. I don't know why you're going along with this, but this little joke has gone on long enough. What's the point? Is Vee giving me some kind of strange test? Is she that insecure?"

Jim just stared at him with confusion. "What are you talking about?"

"Please Jim, just give me a break. The joke's over, ok?"

"I don't know what you mean."

"Swear to me that you guys and Vee aren't playing some trick on me!"

Jim held his hand to his heart. "I swear, man, I don't know what you're talking about!"

"I'm talking about that is not the same woman I've been dating for the past 3 years. The real Vee doesn't look like that at all. Honestly, I was going to break up with her today!"

Jim looked at him, "Do you still want to break up with her?"

"Well, I want to solve this mystery. But it's hard to break up with Vee now that she's so good looking!"

Jim laughed. "Maybe you're the one that's changed! It sounds like you're losing your mind! Maybe you should go to a doctor."

After a complete health check that included a CAT scan, an MRI, and blood tests, doctors said he was in physical health. But what about his mental health?

John went to a psychologist who seemed quite amused at his story.

"Not the most tragic case, you have to admit."

"Is there some way you can explain this? Could it be a tumor or could I just be losing my mind?"

"John, instead of worrying about how things are wrong, why don't you try to focus on what's going right. Isn't this something you say you'd wished for?"

That was true.

"There's something else that's bugging me. I almost never used to get jealous. It was always Vee that was jealous of me, probably because she lacked confidence in herself.

"But now...everywhere we go, she stops the room. And it's not the guy's looks that are the worst. It's the girls that look at her and then me. I know what they're thinking: Why is she with that loser. I'm thinking the same thing too!"

The psychologist took a moment before replying. "So the problem is you. You have the perfect girlfriend, literally, but you just can't get over yourself."

"Exactly. A friend of mine from my college days said something interesting once when I asked why he wasn't into dating girls only for their beauty. He said seven dates is how long it takes to get tired of a beautiful woman that you don't actually get along with. Eventually, you get used to how beautiful they are. Then the insecurity and jealousy begin!"

Chapter 4

John sat her down and explained why he couldn't remain with such a perfect creature.

"It sounds crazy, but you're just too beautiful and perfect. I'm not good enough for you anymore." It wasn't easy to tell her, especially because her beautiful eyes made it so hard to focus.

"You have really changed." Vee said and he couldn't help but laugh.

"If only you knew..."

She tried to fight for answers, but how could he possibly tell her the truth? However, she was persistent, and as always, her beauty made his will weak.

"Ok. I'll tell you what happened" John said. "But you have to promise that you won't say I'm crazy after I explain."

"Then give me a reason that's not crazy. Fair enough?"

"OK. You know how in movies, someone sees something amazing, like a vampire or a zombie or some other monster and no one believe them?"

"Are you a vampire?" she said, somewhat humorously.

"Of course not. But I think you might find that easier to believe."

So, John came out with it all, how she used to look much less attractive than she did now. As he expected, it did not go well.

"You're wrong, actually. I don't think you're crazy, just a jerk for telling such a lame story."

But he'd seen enough movies to know this kind of situation could never go well. Who can really believe that a person could magically change into a new form? So he produced the documents demonstrating the therapy and testing he'd been through.

Vee read for a few minutes in disbelief before throwing the papers on the floor. She gripped her chin with her left hand, staring out the window in her thinking-cap mode, trying to figure out how John could believe this.

"Then you are crazy," she said, "because what you are saying is impossible!"

With that she stormed out. He didn't know if she would return. But he made a wish to myself, he never imagined he would ever make.

John didn't see Vee for a few days after that.

And then one day, he came home from work, and there she was.

It was the old Vee. Short and pudgy, with a flat nose and acne on her cheeks. When she opened her eyes, the biggest change was that they again were small and back to their dull light-brown color. The sparkle that made John feel weak in the knees was gone, but the intelligence and softness that he knew so well was back again, making them the most beautiful eyes he could ever picture. He had missed them. Her bare hands and fingers were just as before, too.

"What can that smile on your face mean?" she asked.

"It worked!"

She sighed and reached for a mirror. "I don't look any different," she said to herself.

"Well. you certainly do to me."

"So now I'm uglier and you're happy. You really are crazy. Lucky for you I love that about you too."

"I love you too! Just please never change again."

John stroked the acne on her cheek. This was not what he wanted, but what he needed. He was not Brad Pitt, and he didn't need a movie star wife. How tiring it had been, he thought. He had felt like keeping a large diamond in the house, always thinking it might be stolen.

But this imperfect form in front of him? She wasn't a jewel to anyone else but him. Maybe there were more important things than beauty.

He thought the look in her eyes matched his own until she tapped John's weak chin.

"You know, I was reading something about chin implants..." she began.

Glossary

to bug: to annoy or bother

confused: having trouble thinking clearly, unsure of what is happening

chin implants: bags that go inside someone's chin to make them more attractive

goofing: making a joke, trying to trick someone

gulliabilty: the quality of being easy to fool or trick

latte: a coffee drink

MRI: a kind of scan that lets doctors look inside your body

After You Read

1. What is narrator doing at the beginning of the story?

2. Why is the narrator confused by the woman talking to him?

3. What do the narrator's friends think about the changes in Vee?

4. Why does the narrator go see doctors?

5. What does the narrator do to solve his problem?

6. How does Vee react?

7. What happens when Vee returns? Is the narrator happy about this?

8.

How does the narrator change throughout the story?

9. What do you think Vee means when she talks about chin implants?

10. What do you think really happened? Did Vanessa really change? Or was it all in the narrator's head?

11. Do you think the narrator was right to handle the situation the way he did?

12. Do you agree that it is hard to date someone who is very beautiful?

13. 'Beauty is on the inside' is a popular expression. What does this mean and do you agree?

Writing

Continue the story.

- Does John change his looks? If so, how do he and Vanessa act after that?
- Do we ever find out what happened to Vanessa?
- Does anyone else in John's life change?

More Readers

Baby Shopping
Changes
Empathy
English Class on Mars
Ghost in My Room
Magic Employment Agency
Rebirth
Attack of the Sleep Demon
The AI Therapist
Thought Police
Time Travel Research: Genghis Khan
Virtual Unreality

AlphabetPublish.com/Book-Category/
Graded-Reader

CPSIA information can be obtained
at www.ICGtesting.com
Printed in the USA
LVHW081754220623
750516LV00004B/546